Anette Bley

And What Comes After a Thousand?

Kane/Miller
BOOK PUBLISHERS

"From the beginning?" asks Otto.

"From the beginning!" Lisa shouts. (Lisa shouts because Otto doesn't hear very well, and he can't stand it when people whisper.)

Otto starts from the beginning.

"ONE is for Lisa, there's only one of you in the whole wide world!"

"TWO is for our two emergency cookies," Lisa continues, "and THREE is for the three very best days of the year: my birthday, your birthday and Christmas!"

"FOUR is for the four corners of your favorite pillow," Otto goes on, "and FIVE is for our legs!"
"Plus your cane," adds Lisa.
"All our legs *plus* my cane. Did we get any farther?"
"SIX was for the tomato plant stakes in your garden. SEVEN was for the days of the week, and EIGHT was for the missing tines in your rake. Did you forget all those?"

TOMATENPFLANSE

"We went all the way up to SIXTEEN," Lisa sighs. Then suddenly, she jumps up and says, "I really want to finally, *finally* be able to say ONE is for a bull's eye on the tin buffalo." She takes the slingshot down from its hook and marches off.

Lisa really wanted a bow and arrows, the kind where the arrows have suction cups so they stick to things. But Otto thought arrows might be easily lost in the garden, so he'd made the slingshot for Lisa instead.

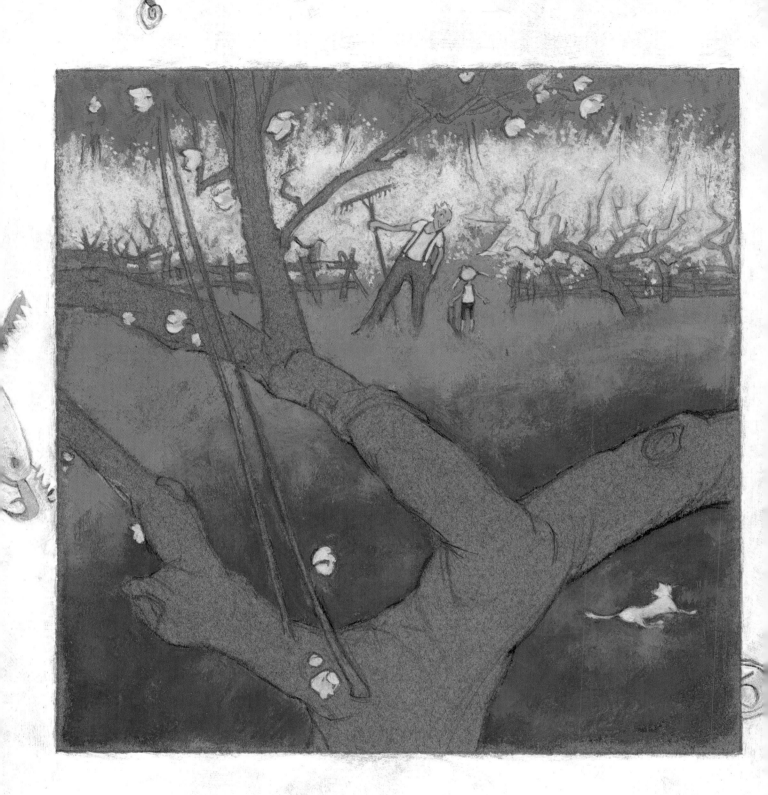

Lisa can shoot pretty well with the slingshot, but she still can't hit the tin buffalo.
She tries again…
"So, did you knock out the buffalo?" Otto asks when she comes back.
"No!" Lisa grumbles. "And I tried at least a thousand times!"

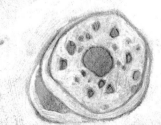

Otto has an idea. He grins slyly and carefully takes the two emergency cookies out of his pocket. "Olga baked these," he says. "I snuck off with them!"
Thank goodness for emergency cookies. They always help.

1 AUS OTTOS HOSENTASCHE

Soon it gets dark. Otto and Lisa watch the first stars appear, one after the other, until the whole sky glitters and gleams.

"How many stars do you think there are?" Lisa asks.

"A thousand," Otto answers, "or maybe even more."

"And what comes after a thousand?" Lisa wants to know.
"One thousand one, one thousand two, one thousand three, one thousand…"
"But don't the numbers ever stop?"
"No, numbers never end."

When Otto rakes the freshly mown grass, it smells sweet and clean.
"This will turn into good soil," he says. Otto knows everything about the garden – that grass turns into earth on the compost heap, how whole trees grow out of the tiniest little seed, and what color the bees' honey will be.
But Lisa can only think about one thing – hitting that buffalo.

6

"Today it has to work!" she says determinedly.

"Did you sneak up on it from the right side yesterday?" Otto asks.

They approach quietly, ducking down in the tall grass. Lisa aims the rust-brown rock, so it's sitting just right in the slingshot and then… *Pow!* … A perfect shot!

"Well, I'll be!" Otto exclaims.

"ONE," Lisa shouts, "ONE is for my first bull's eye on the tin buffalo!" She leaps into the air, and with Otto, dances a great victory dance. Exhausted, they lie back in the grass and look at the sky.

"Otto?" Lisa asks, "How am I supposed to get the dead buffalo to the top of the tree?"
Otto is confused. "Why do you want to put it up there?"

"You told me that some Native Americans used to bury their dead buffalo above ground, in the trees."

Otto laughs. "No, I told you certain tribes sometimes buried *people* above ground, in trees, not buffalo.

"When buffalo were killed it was because their meat was needed for food. They didn't kill them unless they needed to, so they didn't bury them above ground, in trees."

"You look like you could use a little break." Olga always says that when Otto looks tired. Otto and Lisa wink at each other and go into the house.

"FIFTEEN, SIXTEEN, SEVENTEEN," Lisa and Otto count together as they spit the cherry pits onto their plates.

"Exactly SEVENTEEN EACH!" Lisa beams. "Otto, where do numbers come from, anyway?"

Otto thinks for a long time. Finally he says, "I think they're just inside of us…"

Otto hasn't gotten out of bed today. He's tired. Not even the thought of ripe raspberries can lure him into the garden. Lisa picks some for him, but he can't really enjoy them. The next day, and the next day, and the next, he lies in bed, surrounded by pillows, tired and hardly talking at all.

"Will you die soon?" Lisa asks, stroking Otto's hand.

"Mhmmm," Otto nods, "I think so."

"Should we tie you to the top of a tree then?" Lisa wants to know. Otto laughs weakly.
"No, old Otto just wants to be laid to rest in the ground," he says.
"Then I can slowly turn into the soil, just like the grass, remember? And someday flowers
might even grow out of that earth. Imagine that!"
He takes a deep breath. "Yes, I'd like that. To be close to the sky might be nice,
but I'm a gardener."

Sometimes Lisa just holds Otto's hand.

When Otto dies, it is very quiet and still. Olga holds Lisa tight in her arms, and they look at him for a long time. Is he smiling a little? He looks pale. But this time Olga only says quietly, "Goodbye, Otto." And Otto doesn't wink at Lisa.

When Otto is buried, lots of people come. Lisa has never seen some of them before.
Everyone speaks in hushed voices, and they all look terribly serious.
"Don't whisper like that!" Lisa shouts at them. "Otto doesn't like whispering!"
But the strangers just look at her. She goes into the garden to shoot her slingshot.
And guess what? She hits the tin buffalo on her first try!

Lisa runs into the house and does her victory dance, but the strangers still just look at her.
Otto would have danced with her. Finally, Olga comes.
"No one understands," Lisa says quietly. "Why did Otto leave me?"

In the evening, after all the other people have left, Lisa and Olga go into the garden. They sit in the grass and Lisa leans on Olga's shoulder. "The garden isn't beautiful without Otto," Lisa says.

Both of them cry a little until the garden fades to patches of washed-out colors.

"Why did Otto have to leave me?" Lisa asks again.

"Leave you?" Olga thinks about it. "I know it feels that way, but…"

"…I think you just can't see him anymore," she explains.

"What do you mean, can't see him anymore?" Lisa asks. "Do you mean he didn't die?"

"Close your eyes, and imagine a cake!" Olga orders.

Lisa frowns.

"Just do it. Imagine a cake! What do you see?" Olga asks.

"I see a cherry cake with something sprinkled on top and lots of whipped cream."
"What kind of sprinkles? Candied nuts, poppy seeds, rainbow ones?"
"No! Chocolate sprinkles, of course," answers Lisa.
Olga smiles. "You see," she says, "the cake is there, even if you can't see it."

One by one the stars come out.
Lisa thinks of Otto and their five legs in the grass and the two emergency cookies.
He feels close by.
"You know, Olga," she says after a little while,
"Otto is like numbers. He's inside of us, and that will never end."

Kane/Miller Book Publishers, Inc.
First American Edition 2007
by Kane/Miller Book Publishers, Inc.
La Jolla, California

And What Comes After a Thousand?
by Anette Bley
English language edition copyright © 2007 by Kane Miller Book Publishers, Inc.
Title of the original German edition: *Und was kommt nach Tausend?*
Copyright © 2005 by Ravensburger Buchverlag Otto Maier GmbH, Ravensburg (Germany)

All rights reserved. For information contact:
Kane/Miller Book Publishers, Inc.
P.O. Box 8515
La Jolla, CA 92038
www.kanemiller.com

Library of Congress Control Number: 2006931562
Printed and bound in China
1 2 3 4 5 6 7 8 9 10

ISBN: 978-1-933605-27-2